THE ROAD TO BEAR CREEK

BY

ROBERT E. HOWARD

British Library Cataloguing-in-Publication Data
A catalogue record for this book is available from the
British Library

Robert E. Howard

Robert Ervin Howard was born in Peaster, Texas in 1906. During his youth, his family moved between a variety of Texan boomtowns, and Howard – a bookish and somewhat introverted child – was steeped in the violent myths and legends of the Old South. Although he loved reading and learning, Howard developed a distinctly Texan, hardboiled outlook on the world. He became a passionate fan of boxing, taking it up at an amateur level, and from the age of nine began to write adventure tales of semi-historical bloodshed. In 1919, when Howard was thirteen, his family moved to the Central Texas hamlet of Cross Plains, where he would stay for the rest of his life.

At fifteen Howard began to read the pulp magazines of the day, and to write more seriously. The December 1922 issue of his high school newspaper featured two of his stories, 'Golden Hope Christmas' and 'West is West'. In 1924 he sold his first piece – a short caveman tale titled 'Spear and Fang' – for $16 to the not-yet-famous *Weird Tales* magazine. He published with the magazine regularly over the next few years. 1929 was a breakout year for Howard, in that the 23-year-old writer began to sell to other magazines, such as *Ghost Stories* and *Argosy*, both of whom had previously sent him hundreds of rejection slips. In 1930, he began a correspondence with weird fiction master H. P. Lovecraft which ran up to his death six years later, and is regarded as one of the great correspondence cycles in all of fantasy literature.

It was partly due to Lovecraft's encouragement that Howard created his most famous character, Conan the Cimmerian. Conan – a barbarian-turned-King during the Hyborian Age, a mythical period of some 12,000 years ago – featured in seventeen *Weird Tales* stories between 1933 and 1936, and is now regarded as having spawned the 'sword and sorcery' genre, making Howard's influence on fantasy literature comparable to that of J. R. R. Tolkien's. The Conan stories have since been adapted many times, most famously in the series of films starring Arnold Schwarzenegger.

Howard was enjoying an all-time high in sales by the beginning of 1936, but he was also deeply upset by the ill health of his mother, who had fallen into a coma. On the morning of June 11, 1936, he asked an attending nurse whether she would ever recover, and the nurse replied negatively. Howard walked to his car, parked outside the family home in Cross Plains, and shot himself. He died eight hours later, aged just thirty.

When Pap gets rheumatism, he gets remorseful. I remember one time particular. He says to me--him laying on his ba'r-skin with a jug of corn licker at his elbow--he says: "Breckinridge, the sins of my youth is ridin' my conscience heavy. When I was a young man I was free and keerless in my habits, as numerous tombstones on the boundless prairies testifies. I sometimes wonders if I warn't a trifle hasty in shootin' some of the men which disagreed with my principles. Maybe I should of controlled my temper and just chawed their ears off.

"Take Uncle Esau Grimes, for instance." And then pap hove a sigh like a bull, and took a drink, and said: "I ain't seen Uncle Esau for years. Me and him parted with harsh words and gun-smoke. I've often wondered if he still holds a grudge against me for plantin' that charge of buckshot in his hind laig."

"What about Uncle Esau?" I said.

Pap perjuiced a letter and said: "He was brung to my mind by this here letter which Jib Braxton fotched me from War Paint. It's from my sister Elizabeth, back in Devilville, Arizona, whar Uncle Esau lives. She says Uncle Esau is on his way to Californy, and is due to pass through War Paint about August the tenth--that's tomorrer. She don't know whether he intends turnin' off to see me or not, but suggests that I meet him at War Paint, and make peace with him."

3

"Well?" I demanded, because from the way pap combed his beard with his fingers and eyed me, I knowed he was aiming to call on me to do something for him.

Which same he was.

"Well," said pap, taking a long swig out of the jug, "I want you to meet the stage tomorrer mornin' at War Paint, and invite Uncle Esau to come up here and visit us. Don't take no for a answer. Uncle Esau is as cranky as hell, and a peculiar old duck, but I think he'll like a fine upstanding young man as big as you be. Specially if you keep yore mouth shet as much as possible, and don't expose yore ignorance."

"But I ain't never seen Uncle Esau," I protested. "How'm I goin' to know him?"

"He ain't a big man," said pap. "Last time I seen him he had a right smart growth of red whiskers. You bring him home, regardless. Don't pay no attention to his belly-achin'. He's a peculiar old cuss, like I said, and awful suspicious, because he's got lots of enermies. He burnt plenty of powder in his younger days, all the way from Texas to Californy. He was mixed up in more feuds and range-wars than any man I ever knowed. He's supposed to have considerable money hid away somewheres, but that ain't got nothin' to do with us. I wouldn't take his blasted money as a gift. All I want is to talk to him, and git his forgiveness for fillin' his hide with buckshot in a moment of youthful passion.

"If he don't forgive me," said pap, taking another pull at the jug, "I'll bend my .45 over his stubborn old skull. Git goin'."

SO I SADDLED CAP'N KIDD and hit out across the mountains, and the next morning found me eating breakfast just outside War Paint. I didn't go right into the town because I was very bashful in them days, being quite young, and scared of sheriffs and things; but I'd stopped with old Bill Polk, an old hunter and trapper which was camped temporary at the edge of the town.

War Paint was a new town which had sprung up out of nothing on account of a small gold rush right recent, and old Bill was very bitter.

"A hell of a come-off this is!" he snorted. "Clutterin' up the scenery and scarin' the animals off with their fool houses and claims. Last year I shot deer right whar their main saloon is now," he said, glaring at me like it was my fault.

I said nothing but chawed my venison which we was cooking over his fire, and he said: "No good'll come of it, you mark my word. These mountains won't be fit to live in. These camps draws scum like a dead horse draws buzzards. Already the outlaws is ridin' in from Arizona and Utah, besides the native ones. Grizzly Hawkins and his thieves is hidin' up in the hills, and no tellin' how many more'll come in. I'm glad they catched Badger Chisom and his gang after they robbed that bank at Gunstock. That's one gang which won't bedevil us, becaze they're in jail. If somebody'd just kill Grizzly Hawkins, now--"

About that time I seen the stagecoach fogging it down the road from the east in a cloud of dust, so I saddled Cap'n Kidd and left old Bill gorging deer meat and prophecying disaster and damnation, and I rode into War Paint just as the stage pulled up at the stand, which was also the post office and a saloon.

They was three passengers, and none of 'em was tenderfeet. Two was big hard-looking fellows, and t'other'n was a wiry oldish kind of a bird with red whiskers, so I knowed right off it was Uncle Esau Grimes. They was going into the saloon as I dismounted, the big men first, and the older fellow follering them. I touched him on the shoulder and he whirled most amazing quick with a gun in his hand, and he looked at me very suspicious, and said: "What you want?"

"I'm Breckinridge Elkins," I said. "I want you to come with me. I recognized you as soon as I seen you--"

I then got a awful surprise, but not as awful as it would have been if pap hadn't warned me that Uncle Esau was peculiar. He hollered: "Bill! Jim! Help!" and swung his six-shooter against my head with all his might.

Them two fellows whirled and their hands streaked for their guns, so I knocked Uncle Esau flat to keep him from getting hit by a stray slug, and shot one of them through the shoulder before he could unlimber his artillery. The other'n grazed my neck with a bullet, so I perforated him in the arm and again in the hind laig and he fell down across the other'n. I was careful not to shoot 'em in no vital parts, because I seen they was friends of Uncle Esau; but when guns is being drawn it ain't no time to argue or explain.

Men was hollering and running out of saloons, and I stooped and started to lift Uncle Esau, who was kind of groggy because he'd hit his head against a hitching post. He was crawling around on his all-fours cussing something terrible, and trying to find his gun which he'd dropped. When I laid hold on him he commenced biting and kicking and hollering, and I said: "Don't ack like that, Uncle Esau. Here comes a lot of fellers, and the sheriff may be here any minute and 'rest me for shootin' them idjits. We got to get goin'. Pap's waitin' for you, up on Bear Creek."

But he just fit that much harder and hollered that much louder, so I scooped him up bodily and jumped onto Cap'n Kidd and throwed Uncle Esau face-down across the saddle-bow, and headed for the hills. A lot of men yelled at me to stop, and some of 'em started shooting at me, but I give no heed.

I give Cap'n Kidd the rein and we went tearing down the road and around the first bend, and I didn't even take time to change Uncle Esau's position, because I didn't want to get arrested. I'd heard tell them folks in War Paint would even put a fellow in jail for shooting a man within the city limits.

JUST BEFORE WE REACHED the place where I aimed to turn off up into the hills I seen a man on the road ahead of me, and he must have heard the shooting and Uncle Esau yelling because he whirled his horse and blocked the road. He was a wiry old cuss with gray whiskers.

"Where you goin' with that man?" he yelled as I approached at a thundering gait.

"None of your business," I retorted. "Git outa my way."

"Help! Help!" hollered Uncle Esau. "I'm bein' kidnaped and murdered!"

"Drop that man, you derned outlaw!" roared the stranger, suiting his actions to his words.

Him and me drawed simultaneous, but my shot was a split-second quicker'n his'n. His slug fanned my ear, but his hat flew off and he pitched out of his saddle like he'd been hit with a hammer. I seen a streak of red along his temple as I thundered past him.

"Let that larn you not to interfere in family affairs!" I roared, and turned up the trail that switched off the road and up into the mountains.

"Don't never yell like that," I said irritably to Uncle Esau. "You like to got me shot. That feller thought I was a criminal."

I didn't catch what he said, but I looked back and down over the slopes and shoulders and seen men boiling out of town full tilt, and the sun glinted on six-shooters and rifles, so I urged Cap'n Kidd and we covered the next several miles at a fast clip. They ain't a horse in southern Nevada which can equal Cap'n Kidd for endurance, speed and strength.

Uncle Esau kept trying to talk, but he was bouncing up and down so all I could understand was his cuss words, which was free and fervent. At last he gasped: "For God's sake lemme git off this cussed saddle-horn; it's rubbin' a hole in my belly."

So I pulled up and seen no sign of pursuers, so I said: "All right, you can ride in the saddle and I'll set on behind. I was goin' to hire you a horse at the livery stable, but we had to leave so quick they warn't no time."

"Where you takin' me?" he demanded.

"To Bear Creek," I said. "Where you think?"

"I don't wanta go to Bear Creek," he said fiercely. "I ain't goin' to Bear Creek!"

"Yes you are, too," I said. "Pap said not to take 'no' for a answer. I'm goin' to slide over behind the saddle, and you can set in it."

So I pulled my feet outa the stirrups and moved over the cantle, and he slid into the seat--and the first thing I knowed he had a knife out of his boot and was trying to carve my gizzard.

9

Now I like to humor my relatives, but they is a limit to everything. I taken the knife away from him, but in the struggle, me being handicapped by not wanting to hurt him, I lost hold of the reins and Cap'n Kidd bolted and run for several miles through the pines and brush. What with me trying to grab the reins and keep Uncle Esau from killing me at the same time, and neither one of us in the stirrups, finally we both fell off, and if I hadn't managed to catch hold of the bridle as I went off, we'd had a long walk ahead of us.

I got Cap'n Kidd stopped, after being drug for several yards, and then I went back to where Uncle Esau was laying on the ground trying to get his wind back, because I had kind of fell on him.

"Is that any way to ack, tryin' to stick a knife in a man which is doin' his best to make you comfortable?" I said reproachfully. All he done was gasp, so I said: "Well, pap told me you was a cranky old duck, so I reckon the thing to do is to just not notice your--uh--eccentricities."

I looked around to get my bearings, because Cap'n Kidd had got away off the trail that runs from War Paint to Bear Creek. We was west of the trail, in very wild country, but I seen a cabin off through the trees, and I said: "We'll go over there and see can I hire or buy a horse for you to ride. That'll be more convenient for us both."

I started h'isting him back into the saddle, and he said kind of dizzily: "This here's a free country; I don't have to go to Bear Creek if'n I don't want to."

"Well," I said severely, "you oughtta want to, after all the trouble I've went to, comin' and invitin' you. Set still now; I'm settin' on behind, but I'm holdin' the reins."

"I'll have yore life for this," he promised blood-thirstily, but I ignored it, because pap had said Uncle Esau was peculiar.

PRETTY SOON WE HOVE up to the cabin I'd glimpsed through the trees. Nobody was in sight, but I seen a horse tied to a tree in front of the cabin. I rode up to the door and knocked, but nobody answered. But I seen smoke coming out of the chimney, so I decided I'd go in.

I dismounted and lifted Uncle Esau off, because I seen from the gleam in his eye that he was intending to run off on Cap'n Kidd if I give him half a chance. I got a firm grip on his collar, because I was determined that he was going to visit us up on Bear Creek if I had to tote him on my shoulder all the way, and I went into the cabin with him.

There wasn't nobody in there, though a pot of beans was simmering over some coals in the fireplace, and I seen some rifles in racks on the wall and a belt with two pistols hanging on a nail.

Then I heard somebody walking behind the cabin, and the back door opened and there stood a big black-whiskered man with a bucket of water in his hand and a astonished glare on his face. He didn't have no guns on.

"Who the hell are you?" he demanded, but Uncle Esau give a kind of gurgle, and said: "Grizzly Hawkins!"

The big man jumped and glared at Uncle Esau, and then his black whiskers bristled in a ferocious grin, and he said: "Oh, it's you, is it? Who'd of thunk I'd ever meet you here!"

"Grizzly Hawkins, hey?" I said, realizing that I'd stumbled onto the hideout of the worst outlaw in them mountains. "So you all know each other?"

"I'll say we do!" rumbled Hawkins, looking at Uncle Esau like a wolf looks at a fat yearling.

"I'd heard you was from Arizona," I said, being naturally tactful. "Looks to me like they's enough cow-thieves in these hills already without outsiders buttin' in. But your morals ain't none of my business. I want to buy or hire or borrow a horse for this here gent to ride."

"Oh, no, you ain't!" said Grizzly. "You think I'm goin' to let a fortune slip through my fingers like that? Tell you what I'll do, though; I'll split with you. My gang had business over toward Tomahawk this mornin', but they're due back soon. Me and you will work him over before they gits back, and we'll nab all the loot ourselves."

"What you mean?" I asked. "My uncle and me is on our way to Bear Creek--"

"Aw, don't ack innercent with me!" he snorted disgustedly. "Uncle! You think I'm a plumb fool? Cain't I see that he's yore prisoner, the way you got him by the neck? Think I don't know what yo're up to? Be reasonable. Two can work this job better'n one. I know lots of ways to make a man talk. I betcha if we kinda massage his hinder parts with a red-hot brandin' iron he'll tell us quick enough where the money is hid."

Uncle Esau turned pale under his whiskers, and I said indignantly: "Why, you low-lifed polecat! You got the crust to pertend to think I'm kidnapin' my own uncle for his dough? I got a good mind to shoot you!"

"So you're greedy, hey?" he snarled, showing his teeth. "Want all the loot yoreself, hey? I'll show you!" And quick as a cat he swung that water bucket over his head and let it go at me. I ducked and it hit Uncle Esau in the head and stretched him out all drenched with water, and Hawkins give a roar and dived for a .45-90 on the wall. He wheeled with it and I shot it out of his hands. He then come for me wild-eyed with a bowie out of his boot, and my next cartridge snapped, and he was on top of me before I could cock my gun again.

I dropped my gun and grappled with him, and we fit all over the cabin and every now and then we would tromple on Uncle Esau which was trying to crawl toward the door, and the way he would holler was pitiful to hear.

Hawkins lost his knife in the melee, but he was as big as me, and a bear-cat at rough-and-tumble. We would stand up and whale away with both fists, and then clinch and roll around the floor, biting and gouging and slugging, and once we rolled clean over Uncle Esau and kind of flattened him out like a pancake.

Finally Hawkins got hold of the table which he lifted like it was a board and splintered over my head, and this made me mad, so I grabbed the pot off the fire and hit him in the head with it, and about a gallon of red-hot beans went down his back and he fell into a corner so hard he jolted the shelves loose from the logs, and all the guns fell off the walls.

He come up with a gun in his hand, but his eyes was so full of blood and hot beans that he missed me the first shot, and before he could shoot again I hit him on the chin so hard it fractured his jaw bone and sprained both his ankles and stretched him out cold.

THEN I LOOKED AROUND for Uncle Esau, and he was gone, and the front door was open. I rushed out of the cabin and there he was just climbing aboard Cap'n Kidd. I hollered for him to wait, but he kicked Cap'n Kidd in the ribs and went tearing through the trees. Only he didn't head north back toward War Paint. He was p'inted southeast, in the general direction of Hideout Mountain. I jumped on Hawkins' horse, which was tied to a tree nearby, and lit out after him, though I didn't have much hope of catching him. Grizzly's cayuse was a good horse, but he couldn't hold a candle to Cap'n Kidd.

I wouldn't have caught him, neither, if it hadn't been for Cap'n Kidd's distaste of being rode by anybody but me. Uncle Esau was a crack horseman to stay on as long as he did.

But finally Cap'n Kidd got tired of running, and about the time he crossed the trail we'd been follering when he first bolted, he bogged his head and started busting hisself in two, with his snoot rubbing the grass and his heels scraping the clouds offa the sky.

I could see mountain peaks between Uncle Esau and the saddle, and when Cap'n Kidd started sunfishing it looked like the wrath of Judgment Day, but somehow Uncle Esau managed to stay with him till Cap'n Kidd plumb left the earth like he aimed to aviate from then on, and Uncle Esau left the saddle with a shriek of despair and sailed head-on into a blackjack thicket.

Cap'n Kidd give a snort of contempt and trotted off to a patch of grass and started grazing, and I dismounted and went and untangled Uncle Esau from amongst the branches. His clothes was tore and he was scratched so he looked like he'd been fighting with a drove of wildcats, and he left a right smart batch of his whiskers amongst the brush.

But he was full of pizen and hostility.

"I understand this here treatment," he said bitterly, like he blamed me for Cap'n Kidd pitching him into the thicket, "but you'll never git a penny. Nobody but me knows whar the dough is, and you can pull my toe nails out by the roots before I tells you."

"I know you got money hid away," I said, deeply offended, "but I don't want it."

He snorted skeptically and said sarcastic: "Then what're you draggin' me over these cussed hills for?"

"Cause pap wants to see you," I said. "But they ain't no use in askin' me a lot of fool questions. Pap said for me to keep my mouth shet."

I looked around for Grizzly's horse, and seen he had wandered off. He sure hadn't been trained proper.

"Now I got to go look for him," I said disgustedly. "Will you stay here till I git back?"

"Sure," he said. "Sure. Go on and look for the horse. I'll wait here."

But I give him a searching look, and shook my head.

"I don't want to seem like I mistrusts you," I said, "but I see a gleam in your eye which makes me believe that you intends to run off the minute my back's turned. I hate to do this, but I got to bring you safe to Bear Creek; so I'll just kinda hawg-tie you with my lariat till I git back."

Well, he put up a awful holler, but I was firm, and when I rode off on Cap'n Kidd I was satisfied that he couldn't untie them knots by himself. I left him laying in the grass beside the trail, and his language was awful to listen to.

THAT DERNED HORSE had wandered farther'n I thought. He'd moved north along the trail for a short way, and then turned off and headed in a westerly direction, and after a while I heard the sound of horses galloping somewhere behind me, and I got nervous, thinking that if Hawkins' gang had got back to their hangout and he had told 'em about us, and sent 'em after us, to capture pore Uncle Esau and torture him to make him tell where his savings was hid. I wished I'd had sense enough to shove Uncle Esau back in the thicket so he wouldn't be seen by anybody riding along the trail, and I'd just decided to let the horse go and turn back, when I seen him grazing amongst the trees ahead of me.

I headed back for the trail, leading him, aiming to hit it a short distance north of where I'd left Uncle Esau, and before I got in sight of it, I heard horses and saddles creaking ahead of me.

I pulled up on the crest of a slope, and looked down onto the trail, and there I seen a gang of men riding north, and they had Uncle Esau amongst 'em. Two of the men was ridin' double, and they had him on a horse in the middle of 'em. They'd took the ropes off him, but he didn't look happy. Instantly I realized that my premonishuns was correct. The Hawkins gang had follered us, and now pore Uncle Esau was in their clutches.

I let go of Hawkins' horse and reached for my gun, but I didn't dare fire for fear of hitting Uncle Esau, they was clustered so close about him. I reached up and tore a limb off a oak tree as big as my arm, and I charged down the slope yelling: "I'll save you, Uncle Esau!"

I come so sudden and unexpected them fellows didn't have time to do nothing but holler before I hit 'em. Cap'n Kidd ploughed through their horses like a avalanche through saplings, and he was going so hard I couldn't check him in time to keep him from knocking Uncle Esau's horse sprawling. Uncle Esau hit the turf with a shriek.

All around me men was yelling and surging and pulling guns and I riz in my stirrups and laid about me right and left, and pieces of bark and oak leaves and blood flew in showers and in a second the ground was littered with writhing figures, and the groaning and cussing was awful to hear. Knives was flashing and pistols was banging, but them outlaws' eyes was too full of bark and stars and blood for them to aim, and right in the middle of the brawl, when the guns was roaring and men was yelling and horses neighing and my oak-limb going crack! crack! on human skulls, down from the north swooped another gang, howling like hyeners!

"There he is!" one of 'em yelled. "I see him crawlin' around under them horses! After him, boys! We got as much right to his dough as anybody!"

The next minute they'd dashed in amongst us and embraced the members of the other gang and started hammering 'em over the heads with their pistols, and in a second was the damndest three-cornered war you ever seen, men fighting on the ground and on the horses, all mixed and tangled up, two gangs trying to exterminate each other, and me whaling hell out of both of 'em.

Now I have been mixed up in ruckuses like this before, despite of the fact that I am a peaceful and easy-goin' feller which never done harm to man or beast unless provoked beyond reason. I always figger the best thing to do in a brawl is to hold your temper, and I done just that. When this one feller fired a pistol plumb in my face and singed my eyebrows I didn't get mad. When this other 'un come from somewhere to start biting my leg I only picked him up by the scruff of the neck and knocked a horse over with him. But I must of lost control a little, I guess, when two fellers at once started bashing at my head with rifle-butts. I swung at them so hard I turned Cap'n Kidd plumb around, and my club broke and I had to grab a bigger and tougher one.

Then I really laid into 'em.

Meanwhile Uncle Esau was on the ground under us, yelling bloody murder and being stepped on by the horses, but finally I cleared a space with a devastating sweep of my club, and leaned down and scooped him up with one hand

and hung him over my saddle horn and started battering my way clear.

But a big feller which was one of the second gang come charging through the melee yelling like a Injun, with blood running down his face from a cut in his scalp. He snapped a empty cartridge at me, and then leaned out from his saddle and grabbed Uncle Esau by the foot.

"Leggo!" he howled. "He's my meat!"

"Release Uncle Esau before I does you a injury!" I roared, trying to jerk Uncle Esau loose, but the outlaw hung on, and Uncle Esau squalled like a catamount in a wolf-trap. So I lifted what was left of my club and splintered it over the outlaw's head, and he gave up the ghost with a gurgle. I then wheeled Cap'n Kidd and rode off like the wind. Them fellows was too busy fighting each other to notice my flight. Somebody did let bam at me with a Winchester, but all it done was to nick Uncle Esau's ear.

THE SOUNDS OF CARNAGE faded out behind us as I headed south along the trail. Uncle Esau was belly-aching about something. I never seen such a cuss for finding fault, but I felt they was no time to be lost, so I didn't slow up for some miles. Then I pulled Cap'n Kidd down and said: "What did you say, Uncle Esau?"

"I'm a broken man!" he gasped. "Take my secret, and lemme go back to the posse. All I want now is a good, safe prison term."

"What posse?" I asked, thinking he must be drunk, though I couldn't figure where he'd got any booze.

"The posse you took me away from," he said. "Anything's better'n bein' dragged through these hellish mountains by a homicidal maneyack."

"Posse?" I gasped wildly. "But who was the second gang?"

"Grizzly Hawkins' outlaws," he said, and added bitterly: "Even they would be preferable to what I been goin' through. I give up. I know when I'm licked. The dough's hid in a holler oak three miles south of Gunstock."

I didn't pay no attention to his remarks, because my head was in a whirl. A posse! Of course; the sheriff and his men had follered us from War Paint, along the Bear Creek trail, and finding Uncle Esau tied up, had thought he'd been kidnaped by a outlaw instead of merely being invited to visit his relatives. Probably he was too cussed ornery to tell 'em any different. I hadn't rescued him from no bandits; I'd took him away from a posse which thought they was rescuing him.

Meanwhile Uncle Esau was clamoring: "Well, why'n't you lemme go? I've told you whar the dough is; what else you want?"

"You got to go on to Bear Creek with me--" I begun; and Uncle Esau give a shriek and went into a kind of convulsion, and the first thing I knowed he'd twisted around and jerked my gun out of its scabbard and let bam! right in my face so close it singed my hair. I grabbed his wrist and Cap'n Kidd bolted like he always does when he gets the chance.

"They's a limit to everything!" I roared. "A hell of a relative you be, you old maneyack!"

We was tearing over slopes and ridges at breakneck speed and fighting all over Cap'n Kidd's back--me to get the gun away from him, and him to commit murder. "If you warn't kin to me, Uncle Esau, I'd plumb lose my temper!"

"What you keep callin' me that fool name for?" he yelled, frothing at the mouth. "What you want to add insult to injury--" Cap'n Kidd swerved sudden and Uncle Esau tumbled over his neck. I had him by the shirt and tried to hold him on, but the shirt tore. He hit the ground on his head and Cap'n Kidd run right over him. I pulled up as quick as I could and hove a sigh of relief to see how close to home I was.

"We're nearly there, Uncle Esau," I said, but he made no comment. He was out cold.

A short time later I rode up to the cabin with my eccentric relative slung over my saddle-bow, and took him and stalked into where pap was laying on his b'ar-skin, and slung my burden down on the floor in disgust. "Well, here he is," I said.

Pap stared and said: "Who's this?"

"When you wipe the blood off," I said, "you'll find it's your Uncle Esau Grimes. And," I added bitterly, "the next time you want to invite him to visit us, you can do it yourself. A more ungrateful cuss I never seen. Peculiar ain't no name for him; he's as crazy as a locoed jackass."

"But that ain't Uncle Esau!" said pap.

"What you mean?" I said irritably. "I know most of his clothes is tore off, and his face is kinda scratched and skinned and stomped outa shape, but you can see his whiskers is red, in spite of the blood."

"Red whiskers turn gray, in time," said a voice, and I wheeled and pulled my gun as a man loomed in the door.

It was the gray-whiskered old fellow I'd traded shots with on the edge of War Paint. He didn't go for his gun, but stood twisting his mustache and glaring at me like I was a curiosity or something.

"Uncle Esau!" said pap.

"What?" I hollered. "Air you Uncle Esau?"

"Certainly I am!" he snapped.

"But you warn't on the stagecoach--" I begun.

"Stagecoach!" he snorted, taking pap's jug and beginning to pour licker down the man on the floor. "Them things is for wimmen and childern. I travel horse-back. I spent last night in War Paint, and aimed to ride on up to Bear Creek this mornin'. In fact, Bill," he addressed pap, "I was on the way here when this young maneyack creased me." He indicated a bandage on his head.

"You mean Breckinridge shot you?" ejaculated pap.

"It seems to run in the family," grunted Uncle Esau.

"But who's this?" I hollered wildly, pointing at the man I'd thought was Uncle Esau, and who was just coming to.

"I'm Badger Chisom," he said, grabbing the jug with both hands. "I demands to be pertected from this lunatick and turned over to the sheriff."

"HIM AND BILL REYNOLDS and Jim Hopkins robbed a bank over at Gunstock three weeks ago," said Uncle Esau; the real one, I mean. "A posse captured 'em, but they'd hid the loot somewhere and wouldn't say where. They escaped several days ago, and not only the sheriffs was lookin' for 'em, but all the outlaw gangs too, to find out where they'd hid their plunder. It was a awful big haul. They must of figgered that escapin' out of the country by stage coach would be the last thing folks would expect 'em to do, and they warn't known in this part of the country.

"But I recognized Bill Reynolds when I went back to War Paint to have my head dressed, after you shot me, Breckinridge. The doctor was patchin' him and Hopkins up, too. The sheriff and a posse lit out after you, and I follered 'em when I'd got my head fixed. Course, I didn't know who you was. I come up while the posse was fightin' with Hawkins' gang, and with my help we corralled the whole bunch. Then

I took up yore trail again. Purty good day's work, wipin' out two of the worst gangs in the West. One of Hawkins' men said Grizzly was laid up in his cabin, and the posse was goin' to drop by for him."

"What you goin' to do about me?" clamored Chisom.

"Well," said pap, "we'll bandage yore wounds, and then I'll let Breckinridge here take you back to War Paint--hey, what's the matter with him?"

Badger Chisom had fainted.